T0197621

EL REGALO DE YUKIYÚ

Lizzette Delgado

© 2020 Lizzette Delgado. All rights reserved.

No part of this book may be reproduced, stored in a retrieval system, or transmitted by any means without the written permission of the author.

AuthorHouse™
1663 Liberty Drive
Bloomington, IN 47403
www.authorhouse.com
Phone: 1 (833) 262-8899

Because of the dynamic nature of the Internet, any web addresses or links contained in this book may have changed since publication and may no longer be valid. The views expressed in this work are solely those of the author and do not necessarily reflect the views of the publisher, and the publisher hereby disclaims any responsibility for them.

This book is printed on acid-free paper.

ISBN: 978-1-6655-0377-8 (hc)
ISBN: 978-1-7283-4507-9 (sc)

Library of Congress Control Number: 2020901957

Print information available on the last page.

Published by AuthorHouse 12/17/2020

author HOUSE®

I dedicate this book to the Creator
who blessed us with our beautiful
island Borinquen: as well to my
beloved family and wonderful friends.
I also want to give a special thanks
to my friend Elizabeth Bowden
for her translation of my book.

*Dedico este libro al Creador que
Vistió de gala a mi hermosa isla
Borinquen: también a mi amada familia
y a mis queridas amistades. También
quiero agradecer especialmente
a mi amiga Elizabeth Bowden
por su traducción de mi libro.*

EL REGALO DE YUKIYÚ

(The gift of Yukiyú)

English Version

As legend tells, thousands of years ago the brilliant colors of a beautiful rainbow adorned a tiny island called Borinquen.

As if by magic, its inhabitants, the native Tainos, witnessed before their eyes the formation of a beautiful forest full of brilliantly-colored birds and mountains so tall they almost touched the sky.

Everything was perfect – MARVELOUS! They marveled at the dense, leafy trees and flowers, the beautiful stream that flowed from the heart of the mountain and fell at their feet as if joining in prayer.

Suddenly, out of nowhere they could hear a beautiful melody... "Coquí, coqui, coqui..." Surprised, they looked around to try and find from where this glorious sound was coming.

It wasn't the birds. It wasn't the other animals. It couldn't be the trees, nor the plants, nor the stream. What could it be? From where was the sound coming?

Suddenly everything was basked in a brilliant light, and an enormous figure spoke to the Tainos.

"I am Yukiyu, the god of this forest. I have created it for you all to enjoy."

"The music you hear is my gift to you. It comes from a tiny frog, so tiny that there is no other like him in all the world. His name is Coqui. He will accompany you every night and every day of your lives. For no reason will he leave this place because he would not survive."

From that point on, the Tainos named the beautiful forest "El Yunque" in honor of their god, Yukiyu.

All the days of their lives, the Tainos, accompanied by the melodious song of the Coqui, cared diligently for El Yunque, giving thanks to Yukiyu for such a lovely gift.

EL REGALO DE YUKIYÚ

Versión en español

Cuenta la leyenda que hace miles de años un hermoso arco iris vistió con sus brillantes colores a una pequeña isla llamada Borinquen.

Como si fuera por arte de magia, sus habitantes los indios taínos fueron testigos de como se formó antes sus ojos un hermoso bosque con aves de preciosos colores y montañas tan altas y tan altas que casi tocaban el cielo.

Todo era perfecto; maravilloso. Estaban extáticos con los frondosos árboles, con las flores, con el hermoso riachuelo que brotaba del corazón del monte y caía a sus pies como una alabanza.

De repente, de la nada se escuchó una hermosa melodía... "coquí, coquí, coquí..." Todos se miraron extrañados tratando de encontrar de dónde venía aquel sonido glorioso.

No eran la aves. No eran los otros animales.
No podían ser los árboles, ni las plantas,
ni el río. ¿Qué será? ¿De dónde vendrá?

De repente todo se convirtió en una brillante luz y una figura gigantesca les habló a los indios.

"Yo soy Yukiyú, el dios de este bosque. Lo he creado para que ustedes disfruten de él."

"La música que escuchan es mi regalo para ustedes. Es una ranita pequeña. Tan pequeña que no hay en el mundo otra igual. Su nombre es Coquí. Él los acompañará todas las noches y todos los días de sus vidas. Por ningún motivo debe salir de aquí porque morirá."

Desde estonces los indios taínos llamaron
al hermoso bosque El Yunque en honor a
su dios Yukiyú.

Todos los días de sus vidas los indios acompañados de la melodiosa canción del Coquí cuidan afanosamente a El Yunque, dándole siempre las gracias por tan hermoso regalo al dios de las montañas Yukiyú.

ABOUT THE ILLUSTRATOR

Danny Torres was born in Adjuntas, a little town in the middle of Puerto Rico. Danny, a self-taught multidisciplinary artist has been living in Philadelphia since 1988. Since then he has been teaching art classes in community center and schools from around the city. He has also been involved in design and development of murals around the state of Pennsylvania with organizations like Creative Artist Network, Philadelphia Mural Program, Taller Puertoriqueño, SEPTA, Pennsylvania State Museum Concilio or Spanish-speaking organizations and the Puerto Rican cultural centers in Chicago, Philadelphia, Hartford and New York. His artworks are in private and public collections to mention some, HACE (Hispanic association of hispanic enterprises), Nueva Esperanza Inc., Borinquen Credit Union, Casapueblo, Inc., Pennsylvania State Museum and others.

As an educator, Danny Torres has been teaching the technique of Vegigante mask making, the folkloric character mask is used by the artist to teach his students the importance of keeping alive the Boricua-Latino cultural heritage in their hearts and lives. Other artistic disciplines Danny has been working on are theater, writing, performance art and dance.

Printed in the United States
By Bookmasters